This book is a brief retelling of the famous tale of THE WIZARD OF OZ. Specially designed for very young children, it takes them along the same yellow brick road that has brought generations of children into the sparkling land of Oz. Here they will meet the beloved Dorothy and her companions—the Scarecrow, the Tin Woodman, the Cowardly Lion—as well as unforgettable characters like the Munchkins and the Wicked Witch of the West, and finally, the Great and Terrible Wizard himself.

THE WIZARD OF OZ

By L. FRANK BAUM

Adapted by ALLEN CHAFFEE

Illustrated by ANTON LOEB

Prepared under the supervision of JOSETTE FRANK,
Children's Book Adviser of the Child Study Association of America

RANDOM HOUSE · NEW YORK

This title was originally cataloged by
the Library of Congress as follows:

Baum, Lyman Frank, 1856–1919.   The Wizard of Oz; adapted
by Allen Chaffee, illustrated by Anton Loeb. Prepared under the
supervision of Josette Frank. New York, Random House [1950]
63 p. illus. (part col.) 29 cm.   I. Chaffee, Allen. II. Title.

PZ8.B327Wh 12   50–10602

ISBN: 0-394-80689-1   0-394-90689-6 (lib. bdg.)

"CYCLONE COMING!" Uncle Henry shouted. "I'll go look after the stock."

"Quick, Dorothy!" Aunt Em screamed. "Run for the cellar!"

But Dorothy ran to get Toto, her little dog. He had jumped out of her arms and was hiding under the bed. Aunt Em threw open the trap-door in the floor and climbed down the ladder into the small, dark hole. Dorothy caught Toto at last, and started toward the trap-door to follow her aunt.

Suddenly there came a great shriek from the wind. The house shook so hard that Dorothy lost her footing and found herself sitting on the floor.

Then a strange thing happened. The house whirled around two or three times and rose slowly through the air. Dorothy felt dizzy as it rocked and swayed.

It was very dark, and the wind howled horribly around her, but soon the house seemed to be gliding more easily.

Hour after hour passed. At last Dorothy crawled over the swaying floor to her bed and lay down. Toto kept close to her. And then Dorothy fell fast asleep.

She was awakened by a great BUMP! Dorothy sat up. The house wasn't moving. And it was no longer dark outside. Sunshine came in at the window. Dorothy and her little dog ran outside.

A little old woman all in sparkling white stood smiling at her. Behind her, three little old men took off their hats and bowed.

"Welcome," the little old woman said, "to the land of the Munchkins. And we are grateful to you for killing the Wicked Witch of the East. You have set us free."

"Did I kill her?" Dorothy could not understand.

"Your house fell on her," replied the little old woman with a laugh; "and that is the same thing." She pointed to a corner of the house.

Dorothy looked. An ugly old Witch, all in black, was just fading away — all but her two feet in silver shoes.

Dorothy was frightened. "Are you a witch?" she asked the little old woman.

"Yes; but I am a good witch. I am the Witch of the North," the little old woman told her. "The Witch of the South is good, too. Your house fell on one of the bad witches. And now there is only one wicked witch left in the Land of Oz—the one who lives in the West."

"But Aunt Em said there were no witches any more," Dorothy told her.

"Who is Aunt Em?" asked the Witch of the North.

"She lives in Kansas, and I live with her," Dorothy told her sadly. "Or I did."

"Is Kansas a civilized country?"

"Oh, yes," replied Dorothy.

"Then that accounts for it!" the Witch of the North said. "I've heard there were no witches left in civilized countries. But, you see, The Land of Oz has never been civilized. So it still has witches and wizards."

"What are wizards?" Dorothy wanted to know.

The Witch whispered, "Oz himself is the Great Wizard. He lives in the City of Emeralds."

Dorothy was going to ask another question, but just then the Munchkins, who had been standing silently by, gave a shout and pointed. Dorothy and the Witch of the North looked. The feet of the dead Witch had disappeared entirely and nothing was left but the silver shoes.

The little old woman handed the shoes to Dorothy. "Why don't you wear them, dear? We think they may have a magic charm. But we don't know what it is."

Dorothy tried them on. They were a perfect fit. Then she said to the Munchkins:

"I want to get back to my aunt and uncle. I'm sure they are worried about me. Can you help me find my way?"

They all shook their heads.

The first Munchkin pointed. "To the East lies a great desert."

The next Munchkin pointed. "To the South, the woods are full of wild beasts."

The third Munchkin pointed. "The West, where the yellow Winkies live, is ruled by the Wicked Witch of the West. She would make you her slave if you passed her way."

The little old woman took off her pointed cap and balanced it on the tip of her nose. "One, two, three," she counted. "Tell us which way Dorothy goes."

The cap suddenly changed to a slate. On it was printed:
"LET DOROTHY GO TO THE CITY OF EMERALDS."

The little old woman spoke. "There! Now you know where to go. Perhaps Oz, the Great Wizard, will help you."

"How can I get there?" Dorothy asked, picking up Toto.

"You must walk," the little old woman told her. "It's a long, long journey. But just follow the yellow brick road."

The three Munchkins bowed to Dorothy. "Have a pleasant journey," they said.

The little old woman kissed her on the forehead. "No one will dare to hurt a person with my kiss on her forehead," she said. And where her lips had touched, they left a shining mark. Then the Witch whirled three times on one heel—and was gone!

Dorothy started along the yellow brick road, and Toto followed. The silver shoes tinkled gaily as the little girl walked.

She had not gone far when she came to a cornfield She saw a Scarecrow placed high on a pole to keep the birds away from the ripe corn. He waved one arm at her and called out, "I'm tired of being up here."

"Can't you get down?" Dorothy called.

"No, because this pole is stuck up my back. Will you please take the pole away?"

Dorothy lifted him off the pole.

"Thanks," he said. "If I had any brains, I'd have thought of a way myself."

"Haven't you any brains?" Dorothy asked in surprise.

"No. You see, I'm stuffed, so I have no brains at all," he told her sadly.

"Then come with me," Dorothy urged, "and I'll ask the Wonderful Wizard of Oz to give you some brains."

Little Toto sniffed at the Scarecrow.

"Don't mind Toto," Dorothy told her new friend. "He never bites."

"Oh, I'm not afraid," replied the Scarecrow. "I couldn't feel it if he did. The only thing I'm afraid of is a lighted match."

They hadn't gone far when they came to a great forest. And there, holding up an axe, stood a Woodman all made of tin. He groaned, and tried to speak; but his jaws were rusty.

"You poor thing!" Dorothy looked around till she found his oil can. "There!" She oiled his jaws.

The Woodman gave a creak and a squeak before he could speak. "That's better. Now oil my elbow," he begged. "I have not been able to bend that arm for more than a year. All my joints are rusted."

Dorothy oiled his arms and legs.

The Tin Woodman gave a great sigh of relief and lowered his axe.

He told his story. "Once I was a real man, with a warm heart. And I loved a girl. But the Wicked Witch of the East wanted to keep her a slave. She didn't want us to marry. So she laid an evil spell on my axe."

"That axe?" Dorothy breathed.

"Yes." The Tin Woodman swung it at the tree and cut off a branch. "First, it cut off my leg. I had to find a tinsmith who could make me a new leg. Then it cut off my other leg. The tinsmith made me a new one. Next, the axe cut off my arms. The tinsmith made me some new ones. And when the axe cut off my head, he made me a new one. And so it went with the rest of me. But alas, the tinsmith couldn't make me a heart, and without a heart I lost my love for the Munchkin girl."

"Come with me," said Dorothy, "and ask Oz to give you a heart so you can marry the Munchkin maiden."

So the three of them set out—Dorothy, the Scarecrow, and the Tin Woodman—with little Toto trotting alongside.

On—and on—and on they went, down the yellow brick road—to see the Wonderful Wizard of Oz.

NOW DOROTHY and her friends were walking through a deep woods. The road was still of yellow brick. But dry leaves and branches strewed their way. Now and then they heard a growl from some beast hidden among the trees. Dorothy's heart beat fast with fear.

"How long will it be," she asked the Tin Woodman, "before we are out of the forest?"

"I don't know, for I have never been to Emerald City," he told her. "But my father went there once, and he said it was a long way."

Suddenly they heard a loud roar. A Lion bounded into the road.

With one blow of his paw, he knocked the Scarecrow over.

Then he struck the Tin Woodman with his claws. The Woodman fell down, and lay still.

Little Toto barked at the Lion.

The great beast opened his mouth, and showed his sharp teeth.

Dorothy rushed forward and slapped the Lion on his nose.

"Don't you bite Toto!" she cried. "For shame! A big beast like you, to bite a poor little dog!"

"I didn't bite him," the Lion pointed out.

"No, but you tried to," she told him. "You are nothing but a big coward!"

"I know it," said the Lion, hanging his head.

"And to think of your striking a straw man!" Dorothy scolded, as the Scarecrow got to his feet.

"Is he straw? So that's why it was easy!" the Lion said. "Is the other one stuffed too?"

"No, he's made of tin," Dorothy told him, as the Woodman got to his feet.

"So that's why he nearly blunted my claws!" the Lion said. "And is that little thing made of tin?"

"No," Dorothy told him. "Toto is a real dog."

The Lion spoke sadly. "I *am* a coward or I wouldn't have tried to bite such a little thing."

"What makes you a coward?" Dorothy asked him. For the Lion was as big as a small horse.

"I don't know." The Lion wiped away a tear with the tip of his tail. "A Lion is supposed to be the King of Beasts. But I'm so scared of everything!"

"That isn't right," said the Scarecrow. "The King of Beasts is supposed to have courage."

"Perhaps the great Oz could give you courage. Come with us," Dorothy invited him. "We are going to see the Wizard of Oz."

"I will," the Lion agreed.

Again they set off along the yellow brick road. The Lion walked at Dorothy's side.

Once the Tin Woodman stepped on a beetle. It made him very unhappy, for he was always careful not to hurt any living creature, and he began to weep. The tears would have rusted his jaws, but luckily the Scarecrow prevented this by oiling them.

After a while they came to a field of big red poppies. The smell of the flowers was so strong it made Dorothy sleepy. She yawned and lay down.

"Get up!" The Woodman pulled her to her feet. "If you stay here you will sleep forever."

For a time she walked between the Woodman and the Scarecrow. Then she fell fast asleep. Toto lay down beside her.

The Scarecrow and the Woodman made a chair of their hands, and carried Dorothy and Toto.

Because they were not made of flesh, the Woodman and the Scarecrow were not bothered by the smell of the flowers. But the Lion yawned.

"Run fast!" the Scarecrow told him. "If *you* fall asleep you're too big to be carried."

So the Lion ran to get out of the poppy field.

The Scarecrow and the Woodman walked on toward the road. They passed the Lion; he was fast asleep.

"He'll sleep forever," they said sadly.

Once they were out of the poppy field, they carried Dorothy to a pretty spot beside the river and waited for the breeze
to waken her.

"We can't be far from the yellow brick road," the Scarecrow
said.

"Yeow!" A strange beast came leaping toward them. It was
a wildcat. It was chasing a little gray field-mouse.

The Woodman raised his axe and killed the wildcat.

The little mouse squeaked, "Oh, thank you! You have
saved my life."

"I try to help anyone who needs a friend," the Woodman
said. "Even if it's only a mouse."

"Only a mouse!" cried the little animal. "I am a Queen!
Queen of all the field-mice!"

The Woodman bowed.

Three mice came running. "Oh, your Majesty!" they cried. "We thought you'd be killed!" And they bowed so low they almost stood on their heads.

"This tin man saved my life. So we must all obey his wishes," said the little Queen.

"What can *we* do?" they asked.

"Maybe you can save the Lion," the Scarecrow told them. "He's asleep in the poppy field."

"A Lion!" The little Queen shook with fright. "He'd eat us all up!"

"Oh, no;" said the Scarecrow; "this Lion is a coward."

"What shall we do?" the little Queen asked bravely.

"How many mice call you Queen?" the Scarecrow asked her.

"Oh, thousands," she told him.

"Then send for them all," he bade her. "And tell each one to bring a piece of string."

He turned to the Woodman. "Now if you will cut down some trees, we will make a truck."

The Tin Woodman set to work with his axe.

Now the mice came running from all sides. And each had a piece of string in its mouth.

Dorothy awoke, surprised.

"Her Majesty, the Queen!" the Scarecrow introduced them.

Next, he helped the Woodman harness the mice to the truck. When they had thousands of mice all pulling, the truck began to move.

The Scarecrow and the Woodman rolled the Lion onto it. Then they pushed from behind.

Between them all, they got the Lion out of the danger zone.

Dorothy thanked the little Queen and her helpers.

"Goodbye!" they all squeaked, and scampered home.

24

The Scarecrow picked some fruit for Dorothy, for she was hungry.

At last the Lion woke up. And now they started on again to find the Wizard of Oz.

Soon they noticed a beautiful green glow in the sky. They were approaching Emerald City.

In time they came to a big gate all studded with emeralds. They rang the bell, and a little man dressed in green answered.

"We have come," Dorothy told him, "to see the Great Oz."

"First," said the Guardian of the Gate, "you must put on glasses. The brightness of Emerald City would blind you."

So he fitted green glasses on Dorothy, the Scarecrow, the Woodman, the Lion, and even on little Toto. Then he put on his own glasses and said he would show them to the palace.

Emerald City sparkled in the sun. The pavement was green, the houses were green, and even the sky looked green above.

The people all wore green, and had greenish skins. Men with push-carts had green pop-corn for sale.

They came to the palace, where a soldier with a long green beard stood before the door.

"They want to see the Great Oz," the Guardian of the Gates told the soldier.

"Step inside," the Soldier bade them. "Wipe your feet," and he pointed to a green mat.

"Please make yourselves comfortable," he told them now. "I'll tell Oz you are here."

It was a long time before he came back.

"Well, did you see Oz?" Dorothy asked.

"No," the soldier told her. "I have never seen him. No one has. He always sits behind a screen. But he said he'd see you. That is, he will see one of you each day. So, since you'll be here for several days, I'll have you shown to your rooms."

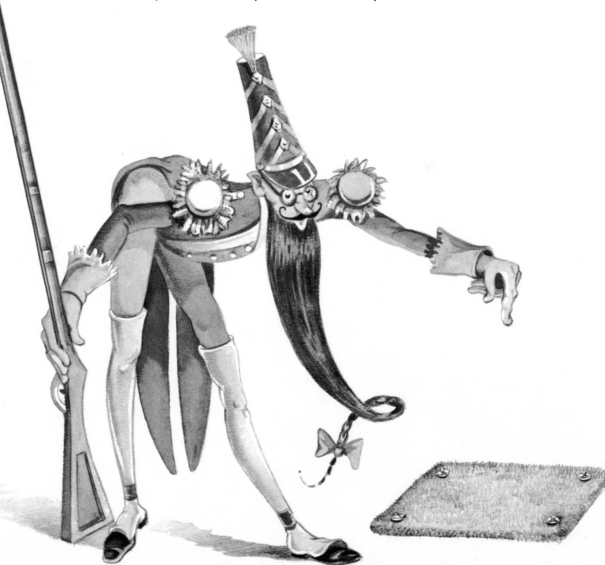

Now a maid with lovely green hair and green eyes led them
through seven hallways and up three flights of stairs. "This
will be your room," she told Dorothy.

The bed had green sheets, and a tiny fountain shot green
perfume into the air.

The maid showed each of them to a room, and the Lion
curled up on his bed like a cat.

Next day Dorothy wore one of the pretty green dresses she found in the closet and went to see Oz.

The Throne Room was round, with a high arched roof. The throne itself was like a chair, but it sparkled with emer-

30

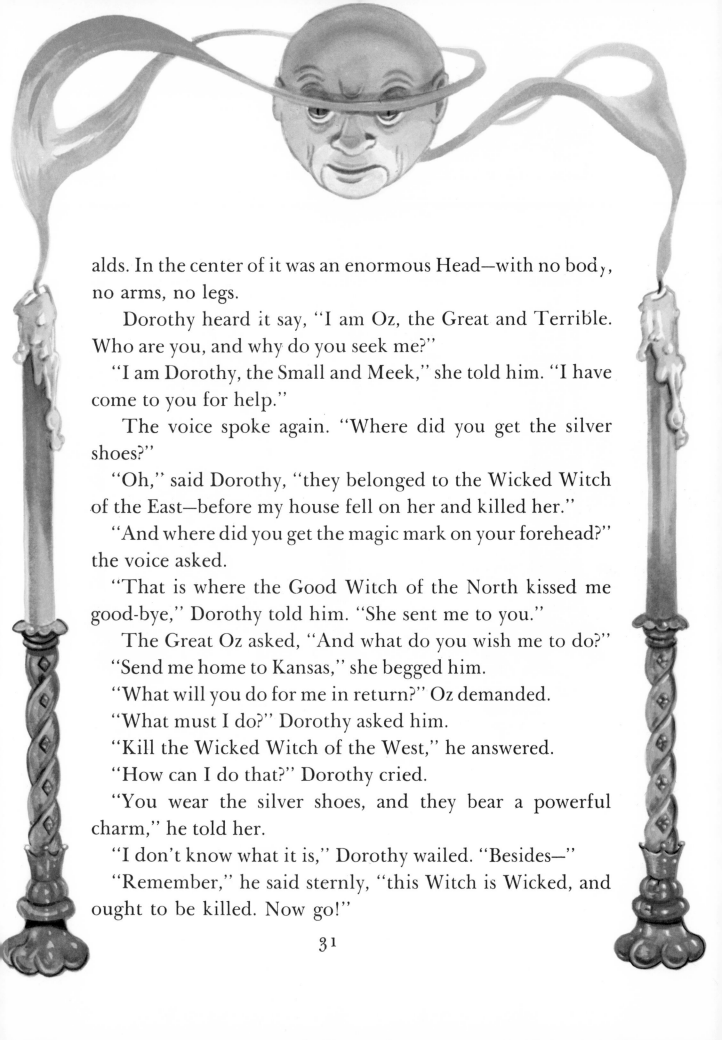

alds. In the center of it was an enormous Head—with no body, no arms, no legs.

Dorothy heard it say, "I am Oz, the Great and Terrible. Who are you, and why do you seek me?"

"I am Dorothy, the Small and Meek," she told him. "I have come to you for help."

The voice spoke again. "Where did you get the silver shoes?"

"Oh," said Dorothy, "they belonged to the Wicked Witch of the East—before my house fell on her and killed her."

"And where did you get the magic mark on your forehead?" the voice asked.

"That is where the Good Witch of the North kissed me good-bye," Dorothy told him. "She sent me to you."

The Great Oz asked, "And what do you wish me to do?"

"Send me home to Kansas," she begged him.

"What will you do for me in return?" Oz demanded.

"What must I do?" Dorothy asked him.

"Kill the Wicked Witch of the West," he answered.

"How can I do that?" Dorothy cried.

"You wear the silver shoes, and they bear a powerful charm," he told her.

"I don't know what it is," Dorothy wailed. "Besides—"

"Remember," he said sternly, "this Witch is Wicked, and ought to be killed. Now go!"

31

Dorothy left the Throne Room, afraid she would never see home again.

Next day, when the Scarecrow was admitted to the Throne Room, there sat a lovely gauze-winged lady all in green. But the voice that came from her lips said: "I am Oz the Terrible. Who are you?"

"I am a Scarecrow stuffed with straw," and he bowed low. "I came to ask if you would put some brains into my head."

"If you will kill the Wicked Witch of the West," the voice told him, "I shall make you the wisest man in the Land of Oz."

The next day the Tin Woodman had his turn. This time a Beast sat on the throne. It was as big as an elephant, and it had five long arms and five legs. Its hair was woolly.

"I AM OZ," it roared. "Who are you?"

"I am a Woodman made of tin," the other said. "I have no heart, and therefore I cannot love. Pray give me a heart, that I may be a man once more."

"Help Dorothy kill the Wicked Witch," said Oz, "and I will give you the biggest heart in the Land of Oz."

The next day the soldier led the Lion to the Throne Room. This time there was nothing to be seen but a Ball of Fire. The Lion backed away.

A low voice sounded. "I am Oz, the Great and Terrible. Who are you?"

"I am a Cowardly Lion," the other said in a small voice. "I am afraid of everything. I beg of you to give me courage."

The Ball of Fire burned fiercely. "Bring me proof," the voice said, "when the Wicked Witch is dead."

The Lion turned tail and rushed from the room.

He told his friends what had happened.

"We must find the Wicked Witch and destroy her," they
decided.

The next day they left Emerald City. At the Gate, the
Guardian took off their green glasses.

"Keep to the West, where the sun sets," he told them.

So on they went, and on—and on—and on.

THE WICKED WITCH had only one eye, but she saw them coming. She was so angry she tore her hair.

In her yellow cupboard, she had a Golden Cap, and this Cap was magic. Whoever owned it could call three times upon the Winged Monkeys, who would obey any order they were given.

Twice already the Wicked Witch had asked their help. First, she had bade them make the little yellow Winkies her slaves.

Second, she had made them drive the Great Oz from the West.

Now she would have her third wish on the Golden Cap. She must stop Dorothy and her friends!

She stood on her left foot, and said:

"Ep-pe, pep-pe, kak-ke!"

She stood on her right foot, and said:

"Hil-lo, hol-lo, hel-lo!"

She stood on both feet, and said:

"Ziz-zy, zuz-zy, zik!"

The earth shook. A low rumbling sound was heard. Then great wings came flapping across the sky. Chitter-chatter, clitter-clatter, a band of great big monkeys flew to the Yellow Castle of the Witch.

37

"What do you command?" their leader asked crossly. "This is the last time you can ever ask anything of us."

"Go destroy those people!" said the Witch. "All but the Lion. Bring him here, so I can harness him like a horse."

Some of the Monkeys dropped loops of rope around the Lion, and flew with him to the Witch's garden, which had a high iron fence.

Others picked up the Tin Woodman, flew high into the air with him, and dropped him on the rocks.

The remaining monkeys pulled all the straw out of the Scarecrow, and threw his clothes into the branches of a tall tree.

The monkey leader had a terrible grin on his face. He reached for Dorothy. But when he saw the mark of the enchanted kiss on her forehead, he drew back.

"She is protected by the Power of Good," he told the others. "We dare not harm her. All we can do is to take her to the Wicked Witch."

The Wicked Witch saw the mark on Dorothy's forehead, too, and knew she dare not harm her. But she thought, "I must try to get her Silver Shoes. She doesn't know their magic."

"Scrub the kitchen floor!" she commanded Dorothy.

Then the old Witch tried to harness the Lion. But he roared so loud, she was frightened.

She decided to starve him. "You'll have nothing to eat until you do as I wish."

But Dorothy took him food at night when everyone was asleep. They tried to plan some way to escape, but it seemed hopeless. The Castle was guarded by the yellow Winkies, who were slaves to the Witch.

Once the old Witch struck Toto and the brave little dog bit her in the leg. The Witch did not bleed, for she was all dried up.

"I must have those Silver Shoes," she told herself. But Dorothy never took them off except when she took a bath. And the old Witch was afraid of water.

At last she thought of a way. She tripped Dorothy and made her fall. One of the Silver Shoes came off.

"Give me my shoe!" Dorothy was angry.

"He, he! It's my shoe now!" The old Witch laughed. "Some day I'll get the other one, too."

"You wicked thing!" Dorothy screamed. In a rage she threw her pail of scrub water at the old Witch.

The witch shrieked with fear. "Stop! Water will be the end of me!" Then she began to melt. Soon there was nothing left of her but a spot on the floor.

Dorothy couldn't believe her good fortune.

She cleaned the Silver Shoe and put it on again, then ran to let the Lion out.

After that Dorothy and the Lion called all the yellow Winkies together to tell them they were free.

"If only the Scarecrow and the Woodman were here," the Lion said, "we could be happy."

"Could you help our friends?" Dorothy asked the Winkies.

"We'll try!"

The little yellow people soon found the Woodman, with his tin all bent. They carried him back to Dorothy.

45

"Are any of you tinsmiths?" she asked.

"Yes, some of us are very good ones," they told her. And soon they had the Woodman looking like himself again.

The Lion wept tears of joy, then wiped his eyes with the tip of his tail.

46

Next, the Winkies found the Scarecrow's clothing in a tall tree. But they couldn't climb it.

The Woodman cut the tree down. Then the Winkies stuffed the clothes with fresh straw and the Scarecrow looked as good as ever. They told him how Dorothy had destroyed the Witch.

"Now we can go back to Oz," the Scarecrow grinned, "and I'll get some brains."

"And I shall get my heart," said the Woodman.

"And I shall get courage," the Lion sighed.

"And I," cried Dorothy, "can go back home to Kansas."

The yellow Winkies wanted the Tin Woodman to stay and be their King, but he had no heart to do it then.

So good-byes were said by everybody.

Then Dorothy went to the Witch's cupboard to fill her basket with food. She saw the Golden Cap, and put it on.

THEY HURRIED back to Emerald City. Word had already reached Oz that the Wicked Witch had melted away.

"We have come to ask you to keep your promise, O Oz," Dorothy told the Voice of the Wizard, when she and her friends found themselves in the Throne Room.

"I must have time to think it over," said the Voice.

At this the Lion thought it might be well to frighten the Wizard, so he gave a loud roar. It frightened Toto, who jumped away, tipping over the screen that stood in a corner. As it fell, Dorothy and the others saw, standing in the spot the screen had hidden, a little, old man with a bald head and a wrinkled face. The Tin Woodman rushed toward him with his axe, crying out:

"Who are you?"

"I am Oz, the Great and Terrible," said the little man in a trembling voice. "But don't strike me, and I'll do anything you want."

"I thought Oz was a great Head," said Dorothy.

"I thought Oz was a lovely Lady," said the Scarecrow.

"I thought Oz was a terrible Beast," said the Tin Woodman.

"I thought Oz was a Ball of Fire," exclaimed the Lion.

"No," said the little man. "I have just been making believe."

"Then you're nothing but a humbug!" cried the Scarecrow.

"That's right," declared the little old man in a pleased voice. And he showed them the Great Head made out of many thicknesses of paper with a carefully painted face. "I hung it from the ceiling by a wire."

"But how about the voice?" Dorothy inquired.

"Oh, I am a ventriloquist." And then he showed them the clothes and the mask he had worn when he seemed to be the lovely Lady. And the Tin Woodman saw that his terrible Beast was nothing but a lot of skins sewn together. The Ball of Fire was only a ball of cotton that burned fiercely when oil was poured on it.

"I was a balloonist with a circus," Oz told them, "and one day the balloon drifted far away. When it came down I found myself in this country. The strange people here, seeing me come from the clouds, thought I was a great Wizard, so I let them think so. And because the country was so lovely, I called it Emerald City. I put green spectacles on all the people so that everything they saw was green."

"But isn't everything here green?" asked Dorothy.

"No. It's only the green spectacles that make it seem so. By the way, I was terribly afraid of those bad Witches, and so pleased when your house fell on one of them. Now that you have melted the other bad Witch, though, I'm ashamed to say I can't keep my promises."

"But you must!" they all cried.

"Well, come and see me tomorrow," Oz said.

Next day the Scarecrow went to the Throne Room.

"I have come for my brains," the Scarecrow remarked uneasily.

"Oh, yes," said Oz. "Excuse me if I have to take your head off, but that's the only way I can fill it with brains."

So he emptied out the straw, and filled the Scarecrow's head with bran—mixed with pins and needles.

"Now you have bran-new brains," he said.

The Scarecrow grinned.

Dorothy looked him over. His head bulged, and needles and pins stuck out in all directions.

"Isn't he sharp?" laughed the Lion.

55

Next, the Woodman went to get his heart.

Oz told him, "I shall have to cut a hole in your chest." This he did, with the tinner's shears. Then he tucked a soft red silk heart into the Woodman's chest.

The Tin Man was greatly pleased.

Then it was the Lion's turn.

The Wizard poured something hot into a saucer.

"What's that?" the Lion asked.

"Well," Oz told him, "when it's inside you, it will be courage. You know courage is always inside one."

The Lion lapped it up.

"How do you feel now?" asked Oz.

"FULL OF COURAGE!" the Lion roared.

The Wizard smiled when he found himself alone. "How can I help being a humbug," he asked himself, "when all these people make me do things that everybody knows can't be done? They already had what they wanted, if they only knew it.—But how can I get Dorothy back to Kansas?"

That evening the Wizard sailed away in a balloon, leaving the Scarecrow to rule over Emerald City, and Dorothy never saw him again.

"Now how will I ever get home?" she cried.

"Let's ask the green soldier," said the Scarecrow. So they did.

"Maybe the Good Witch Glinda can help," the Soldier said.

"Where is Glinda?" they all asked together.

"Go straight South," the soldier told them. "But wild beasts roam the woods."

"No matter. South we go!" The Woodman led the way.

So once again they set out. After a while they came to the woods where the wild beasts roamed. But the Lion roared so loud, no beast came near.

At last they came to the castle where the Good Witch Glinda lived. It was ruby red, and Glinda sat on a ruby throne.

Dorothy told her, "The cyclone blew me to the Land of Oz. How can I get back to Kansas?"

"We'll find a way," Glinda told her. "First give me your Golden Cap."

Dorothy handed it to her.

"Now," said the Good Witch Glinda, "I can ask three favors of the Winged Monkeys."

"They can take the Scarecrow back, to rule over the Emerald City," she decided.

"They can take the Tin Woodman back, to be King of the Winkies.

"They can take the Lion back to the woods, to be King of Beasts."

The Lion and the Woodman and the Scarecrow thanked her, and said good-bye as the Monkeys came.

"But how will I get home to Kansas?" Dorothy begged.
Glinda smiled. "Didn't you know your Silver Shoes have magic power? They will take you anywhere. Just knock the heels together three times, and say where you wish to go."

Dorothy was very happy. Taking Toto in her arms, she said good-bye to everyone.

Then she clapped her heels three times. "Take me home to Aunt Em!" she said.

Whoosh! the wind whistled.

Dorothy found herself sailing through the air. Over woods, over desert, over tall prairie grass she glided.

She landed with a bump.—And there she sat, right in front of the new house Uncle Henry had built. Aunt Em came on the run.

But the Silver Shoes had fallen off, and were lost forever in the desert.

THE WIZARD
OF OZ